THE GREATEST OF ALL

To James
E.A.K.

To Ilil
G.C.

AUTHOR'S NOTE

The source of *The Greatest of All* is "The Wedding Mouse" in Yochiko Uchida's fine collection of Japanese stories, *The Dancing Kettle*. Gerald McDermott's *Stonecutter* is another variation of the same tale. Readers may wish to compare the two, which in classic Zen fashion illustrate the power of patience and humility, but in strikingly different ways. The Stonecutter learns the lesson too late; Father Mouse learns nothing at all, which is why he struck me from the first as a delightfully comical character.

I wish to express my thanks to the graduate students in Portland State University's foreign language department who helped me with the Japanese terms of address. *Otosan* means "Father," *Osama-san* means "Mighty King," and *Ko Nezumi* means—what else?—"Humble Mouse."

Eric A. Kimmel

Text copyright © 1991 by Eric A. Kimmel
Illustrations copyright © 1991 by Giora Carmi
ALL RIGHTS RESERVED
Printed in the United States of America
FIRST EDITION

Library of Congress Cataloging-in-Publication Data
Kimmel, Eric A.
The greatest of all : a Japanese folktale / retold by Eric A. Kimmel
: illustrated by Giora Carmi. —1st ed.
p. cm.
Summary: A mouse father, in search of the mightiest husband for his daughter, approaches the emperor, the sun, a cloud, the wind, and a wall before the unexpected victor finally appears.
ISBN 0-8234-0885-X
[1. Mice—Folklore. 2. Marriage—Folklore. 3. Folklore—Japan.]
I. Karmi, Giora, ill. II. Title.
PZ8.1.K567Gr 1991   90-23658   CIP   AC
398.2—dc 20
[E]

THE
GREATEST
OF ALL

A JAPANESE FOLKTALE

retold by

ERIC A. KIMMEL

illustrated by

GIORA CARMI

Holiday House / New York

Long ago, a family of mice lived in a corner of the emperor's palace.

Father Mouse was a sleek creature with shining fur and stunning whiskers. Because he lived in an emperor's palace, and dined off crumbs from the emperor's table, and dressed in silk from the emperor's wardrobe, he thought himself a splendid mouse indeed!

One day, his pretty daughter Chuko approached him.

"*Otosan*," she began, "a handsome field mouse came by today. His name is *Ko Nezumi*. He wishes to marry me, but he is too shy to ask your permission. Please say yes, *Otosan*. Please!"

Father Mouse pulled at his whiskers.

"My daughter marry a mouse? A humble field mouse! That will never be! You, Chuko, deserve the best. Your husband must be the greatest of all."

"Who is that?" Chuko asked.

"You will see," said Father Mouse. He put on his best silk robe and went to visit the emperor.

"O*sama-san,*" the mouse said, bowing before the emperor. "I bring good news. My daughter Chuko wishes to marry. My wife and I want only the best for her husband. We have chosen you, because you are the greatest of all."

"I am sorry, Father Mouse," the emperor said. "I cannot marry Chuko. There is one who is greater than I."

"Who is that?" the mouse asked.

"The sun," the emperor replied. "When the sun beats hot at noon, even an emperor must seek shade."

"Thank you for telling me," the mouse said. "I will go to the sun."

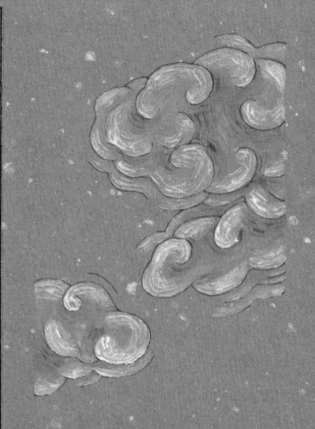

He walked be-yond the palace gate until he came to a broad field. The sun shone high overhead. The mouse looked up and said to the sun, "Sun, I bring good news. My daughter Chuko wishes to marry. My wife and I want only the best for her husband. We have chosen you because you are the greatest of all."

"I am sorry, Father Mouse," the sun said. "I cannot marry Chuko. There is one who is greater than I. His name is Cloud. When Cloud covers the sky, even the sun must hide his face."

"Thank you for telling me," the mouse said. "I will go to the cloud."

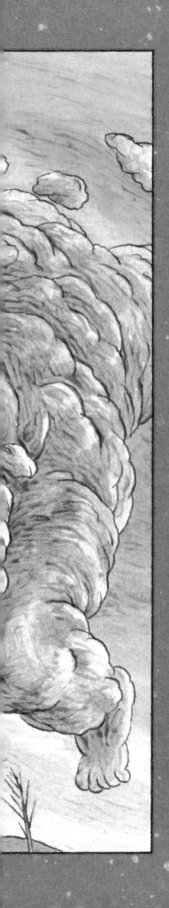

He walked on. A cloud came up and covered the sun. The mouse said to the cloud, "Cloud, I bring good news. My daughter Chuko wishes to marry. My wife and I want only the best for her husband. We have chosen you because you are the greatest of all."

"I am sorry, Father Mouse," the cloud said. "I cannot marry Chuko. There is one who is greater than I. His name is Wind. When Wind blows, clouds scatter."

"Thank you for telling me," the mouse said. "I will go to the wind."

He walked on. The wind blew up and scattered the cloud. The mouse said to the wind, "Wind, I bring good news. My daughter Chuko wishes to marry. My wife and I want only the best for her husband. We have chosen you because you are the greatest of all."

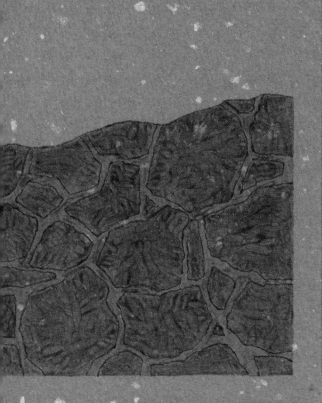

"I am sorry, Father Mouse," the wind said. "I cannot marry Chuko. There is one who is greater than I. His name is Wall. Wall stands firm. I cannot blow him down, no matter how hard I try."

"Thank you for telling me," the mouse said. "I will go to the wall."

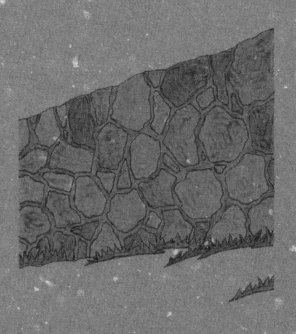

He walked on. After a while he came to the edge of the field, where an ancient stone wall stood. The mouse said to the wall, "Wall, I bring good news. My daughter Chuko wishes to marry. My wife and I want only the best for her husband. We have chosen you because you are the greatest of all."

"I am sorry, Father Mouse," the wall said. "I cannot marry Chuko. There is one who is greater than I. His name is *Ko Nezumi*. He is a humble field mouse. He tunnels inside me, here and there. I can do nothing to stop him. One day he will bring me down."

"I did not know that. Thank you for telling me," said the mouse. He walked along the wall until he came to a tiny door. He knocked. The humble field mouse, *Ko Nezumi,* opened it.

"Father Mouse!" he exclaimed in surprise.

"So you are the famous *Ko Nezumi,*" Father Mouse said. "I came to tell you I have made up my mind. You may marry my daughter Chuko."

So *Ko Nezumi,* the humble field mouse, married pretty Chuko. The sun, the cloud, the wind, the wall, and the emperor came to their wedding. "They make a handsome couple," everyone agreed.

The emperor wrote a haiku poem in their honor:

The very best
Spouse
For a pretty little
Mouse
Is
another
mouse

"I knew it all along," Father Mouse told Mother Mouse that evening before they went to bed. "We mice are the greatest of all!"